Level 1 is ideal for children who have received some initial reading instruction. Stories are told, or subjects are presented very simply, using a small number of frequently repeated words.

Special features:

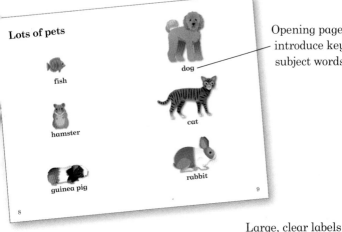

Lots of pets

fish

hamster

guinea pig

dog

cat

rabbit

8

9

Opening pages introduce key subject words

Large, clear labels and captions

Dogs
A dog can be a good pet.

My dog is my friend.

Careful match between text and pictures

Dogs are lots of fun!

11

Educational Consultant: Geraldine Taylor
Book Banding Consultant: Kate Ruttle
Subject Consultant: Dr Kim Dennis-Bryan

LADYBIRD BOOKS

UK | USA | Canada | Ireland | Australia
India | New Zealand | South Africa

Ladybird Books is part of the Penguin Random House group of companies
whose addresses can be found at global.penguinrandomhouse.com.

ladybird.com

First published 2016
001

Copyright © Ladybird Books Ltd, 2016

The moral right of the author and illustrator has been asserted

Printed in China

A CIP catalogue record for this book is available from the British Library

ISBN: 978-0-241-23734-2

Favourite Pets

Written by Catherine Baker

Illustrated by Mark Ruffle

Contents

Lots of pets

fish

hamster

guinea pig

dog

cat

rabbit

Dogs

A dog can be a good pet.

11

Would you like a dog‘

Dogs like to play and jump, and they eat a lot.

Dogs like to eat.

Cats

Cats can be good pets
as well.

cat ——

15

Would you like a cat?

Cats love to jump and play.

My cat loves to play. I can play with her.

They like to sleep a lot,
as well.

My cat likes
to sleep here.

Hamsters

Hamsters like to play.

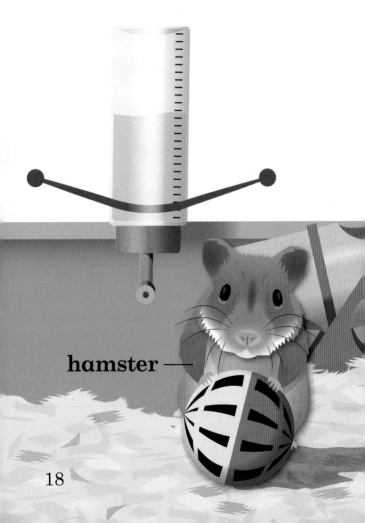

hamster —

They like to sleep a lot, like cats.

My hamster lives in here.

Would you like a pet hamster?

Fish

Fish are fun to watch
and look after.

I help to look after them.

Rabbits

Rabbits love to play,
jump and eat.

rabbit

Would you like a pet rabbit?

23

Guinea pigs

Guinea pigs like to live with a friend.

Guinea pigs love to play.

The guinea pigs love to play in here.

Vets and pets

The vet can help look after our pets.

The vet makes them well.

We love the vet!

27

Picture glossary

 cat

 dog

 eat

 fish

 guinea pig

 hamster

 jump

 rabbit

 sleep

 vet

Index